Mirta Golino

ISBN 0-932529-59-3

All rights reserved. No portion of this publication may be reproduced or transmitted in any form or by
any means, electronic or mechanical, including photocopy, recording, or any information storage and
retrieval system, without permission in writing from the publisher.

© A.B. Curtiss 1997   Printed in Hong Kong   Library bound on acid-free paper

First Edition 10 9 8 7 6 5 4 3 2 1

Curtiss, Arline B.
 Legend of the Giant Pandas/A.B. Curtiss
 p. cm.
 Summary: How the Giant Pandas got their black markings.

ISBN 0-932529-59-3

1. Pandas-Juvenile fiction. 2. Pandas-fiction.
PZ8.3.C8785Le 1997 {E}-dc20 Library of Congress Catalog Card Number: 97-065548

All inquiries to :

OldCastle Publishing
P.O. Box 1193
Escondido, CA 92033
TEL 760-489-0336
FAX 760-747-1198

To my daughter, Sunday, always a good editor for my stories and especially helpful on this one. A.B.C.

To my husband, Michael, and my daughter, Alexis. M.G.

Legend
OF THE
Giant Panda

Written by A. B. CURTISS   Illustrated by MIRTO GOLINO

Oh, the wonder of the Panda that hides in the Bamboo Woods. Oh, the secrets that are whispered by dark wings in rustling leaves, and tracked by footstep along the narrow trails of ancient wilderness. This is a magic place, in a far-away land called China. Here rush the icy rivers where the water dragons swim. Here rise the Mountains of the Sleeping Dragon where the Giant Pandas live.

It is a land of many legends. One legend was told to the Old Pandas in their dreams, that is why they remember it best. So they tell their children about the Great Keeper, a guardian spirit who watches over small bears at night when the sun falls from the sky, and the wind calls itself back home to rest. It is a story that all Pandas know, and now you shall know it too!

The legend says that all Giant Pandas were once absolutely white as snow without any black around their eyes, or their ears, or their paws, or over their shoulders. They had no black fur at all, just like newborn Pandas today. The tiny bears don't get their familiar black markings until several weeks after they are born, a reminder, perhaps, of the mystical change that happened to the first Panda bears long ago.

Mirto Golino

It was so long ago that the Earth was almost all wilderness. Desert dust clouds from elephant herds would drift a mile high into the air. Whole schools of fish would flash like bright pennies on every ocean wave. The mysterious songs of the Great Whales echoed from sea to sea, and the horns and hooves of mighty beasts howled and hammered over the land.

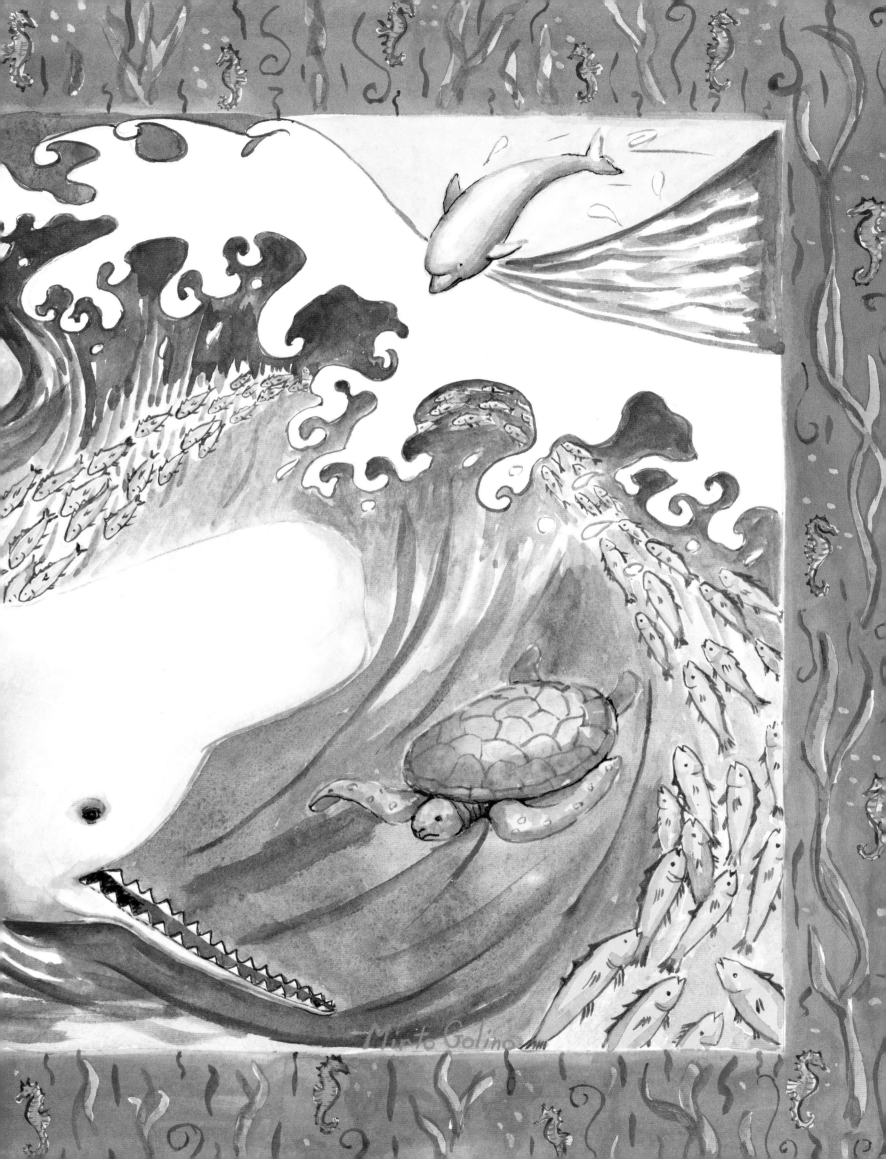

The most wonderful animal of all was the Giant Panda Bear. It was a quiet, peaceful, and secretive creature that was rarely seen outside the dense thickets and caves of the forest where they liked to hide from view. Like pandas today, they too chewed on small sticks of bamboo from morning 'til night. Naturally, the Pandas loved the forest which stretched its kindly branches as far beyond their sight as any of them could imagine.

At the edge of the Panda's forest was a small village where there lived a faithful old Gatekeeper. No one knew where he had come from but he had opened the high village gates at dawn and closed them every evening for as long as anyone could remember. The Gatekeeper loved the Bamboo Woods as much as his friends the Pandas did. It was a deep understanding between them as they each pursued their solitary way through the mountains. They had no need to chatter about it.

At first light every morning the Pandas would watch the Gatekeeper leaning upon the smooth gnarls of his old walking stick as he went about his chores. When they were finished, the old sage would make his daily pilgrimage into the forest. Leaving behind the busyness of the day, he would walk slowly down a small path and disappear into the wall of trees at the edge of the crowded little village. Oh, the best men love the Earth and seek the wisdom of its silent places!

The Gatekeeper loved to wander deep into the woods where the only sound was the chitter of birds, and the flutter of their wings, and the great creak and cracking of tall trees when the wind blew. Sometimes a flurry of dry yellow leaves would suddenly shower down upon him like confetti tossed from the sun. Then the deep lines in his face would soften, like a fond father who smiles upon his children.

The other villagers did not share the old wise man's love for the wilderness. The Gatekeeper would get so angry with the way they cut down the forest to build their houses grander and grander, to dig their gardens wider and wider, and to grow their herds of sheep larger and larger. He would wave his arms about and scold them. He had even been known to grab one or two of the worst offenders by the ear and tweak them good and proper!

Mirto Golino

For the people of the town left great scars upon the mountains, and seemed not to care greatly what they wasted by cutting the thin with the thick if the method was quick enough. They did not care whether or not they left enough bamboo for the Pandas to survive. The villagers foolishly believed that the vast wilderness which surrounded them existed solely for their own disposal and personal profit.

Mirro Gofino

These unwitting town-dwellers were a danger to the forest merely by traveling through it. One day it happened that a farmer made a camp deep in the woods. He built a fire to cook his dinner, keep himself warm, and to keep the snakes and spiders away. He was careless. In the morning after he left, a spark of live fire started up again on its own, and began to lick hungrily at the small sticks and dry leaves on the ground.

The wind blew and the little flames suddenly roared up into a great dragon of hissing and spitting just as the Gatekeeper passed by on his walk. He wrestled the fire dragon to the ground and tried to smother him but, unfortunately, his robe caught on one of the fiery claws. A Giant Panda who rushed to his rescue from nearby was too late to save him. The old Gatekeeper who had loved the forest gave his life trying to save it.

Oh, that was a long and a dark day. All the Pandas now began to fight the fire dragon with great fury. They swatted and patted with their great white arms and stomped with their great white feet until their paws were black with soot. Finally the only flame left in the sky was the last of the evening sun slipping behind the rim of the distant mountains. The fire was out and the fire dragon did not have a single leg left to dance upon, nor one baleful breath of smoke to disturb the clear and starry sky.

It was then the Pandas fully realized that their good friend, the old Gatekeeper, was gone forever. They would never again see his black robe bowing low before the village gates, or track the marks of his old walking stick along the secret paths. They began to weep great Panda tears. They wiped their great Panda eyes with their great fire-blackened Panda paws. They patted each other's shoulders, comforted each other with great sooty Panda hugs, and cupped their ears to distant cries of the other forest creatures who were passing word of the great disaster through the forest.

Mirto Golino

And ever since that day, wherever the Giant Pandas rubbed their fire-blackened paws, on their eyes, their ears, and their shoulders where they hugged each other, they have forever remained black. The Great Spirit of the Wilderness had touched the face of their pain with wonder.

Mirto Golino

The wise old Gatekeeper who had loved and protected the forest was no more. But now all Panda bears would forever carry the shadow of his spirit with them. The black and white markings of the Giant Panda Bears remind all who see them that there is no keeper of the forest but us. And the wilderness, which is the soul of the Earth, is calling. The legend of the Giant Panda is this: the keeper of the forest casts the shadow of a bear.

Mirto Golino

*E*pilogue:

What is true about all legends is that the story changes ever so slightly every time it is told. That is how the old Gatekeeper came to be known finally as the "Great Keeper" mentioned at the beginning of the story.